I0566648

SAMANTHA THE SLEUTH

&

ZACK'S HARD LESSON

SAMANTHA THE SLEUTH

The Case of the Missing Socks

&

ZACK'S HARD LESSON

Learning too Early about Discrimination

BY DAVID H. ROSEN

RESOURCE *Publications* • Eugene, Oregon

SAMANTHA THE SLEUTH
The Case of the Missing Socks
&
ZACK'S HARD LESSON
Learning too Early about Discrimination

Copyright © 2018 David H. Rosen. All rights reserved. Except for brief quotations in critical publications or reviews, no part of this book may be reproduced in any manner without prior written permission from the publisher. Write: Permissions, Wipf and Stock Publishers, 199 W. 8th Ave., Suite 3, Eugene, OR 97401.

Resource Publications
An Imprint of Wipf and Stock Publishers
199 W. 8th Ave., Suite 3
Eugene, OR 97401

www.wipfandstock.com

PAPERBACK ISBN: 978-1-5326-5275-2

Manufactured in the U.S.A.   04/23/18

Illustrations by Diane Katz.

For my parents, Barbara & Max Rosen,
who live on in memory.

PREFACE

Detective work, like being an analyst, involves discovery and compassionate understanding. In the first story, Samantha solves the puzzling question of her missing socks. This story was inspired by my own childhood experience of losing socks.

In Zack's Hard Lesson, he learns about prejudice and how to overcome it through friendship and guidance. This tale is critical for all people to understand what is behind racial discrimination.

David H.Rosen, Eugene, Oregon

SAMANTHA THE SLEUTH

The Case of the Missing Socks

Samantha's socks kept disappearing. Her sock drawer contained nineteen odd socks of various lengths, shapes and colors. Wearing her last pair, Samantha went into her mother's room and said, "I need some new socks. This is the only pair I have left."

Samantha's mother replied, "I'm not buying you any more socks. I've gotten you new ones four times this year. You just keep losing them."

"I don't lose my socks. They disappear."

"Socks don't just disappear," her mom quipped.

Frustrated, Samantha said, "I'm telling you, I'm not losing them. Maybe someone is taking them."

Not looking up from her knitting, Samantha's mother stated firmly, "Now don't be foolish. No one is stealing them. I'm sure they're in your room somewhere. Go look in your drawers, closet, and under and behind your bed."

Samantha was intrigued with the idea that someone might actually be taking her socks. It made sense because this was more than usual sock loss. She scooted away to search her room several times, but came up sock-less.

The search turned up one thing that mystified her. It was a piece of fur. When she showed her mother what she found, her mother said, "That's from one of your furry stuffed animals."

Samantha ran back to her room to check. She examined Pierre the Poodle, Grizzy the Bear, and Willie the Wallaby. But, this fur was not from one of her cuddly friends. She decided to take this fur as a clue. Then, she wondered, "Who would want to take my socks and why?"

The next day after school, Samantha had her usual two cookies with milk. She thought about her missing socks when she gulped down the last drop. The thought came to her when she caught a whiff of her smelly, mismatched socks. She had worn them for three straight days.

Samantha decided to go outside to play basketball. It had rained the night before, but the driveway was dry. She made the first basket. On her second try, the ball hit the rim, bounced away, and rolled into the flower bed by the back door. As she reached down to pick up the ball, Samantha discovered some tracks that she had never seen before. She wondered, "Are those tracks possibly related to my missing socks? Could this be another clue?"

The following day, Katie came over after school. When they finished their snacks, they went out to play in the backyard. They took turns pushing each other on the swing. When Samantha swung high, she noticed something in the grass. She slowed the swing down, jumped off, grabbed Katie's hand and ran over to it. It was a torn up sock!

As soon as Katie went home, Samantha showed the sock to her mother and explained what had happened.

She asked, "How did the ripped up sock get out there?"

Her mother guessed, "Did it fall out of your backpack on the way home from basketball practice?"

Samantha said, "But I was wearing my socks on the way home from practice. Besides, how did it get torn up?"

"Probably a couple of birds pulled it apart and used what they needed for their nest."

Samantha thought this was a good answer, but she knew that she hadn't taken any of her socks outside.

Samantha woke up the next day determined to solve the mystery of the missing socks. She loved to play detective anyway, so it would be fun. She stopped at the library on the way home from school. With the help of Mr. Wilkins, the librarian in the Children's Room, Samantha got out many books on sleuthing.

She learned that most sleuths slouched, looked sleepy and did the bulk of their work at night. Sleuths had hounds with good sniffers that slept with one eye open, keeping a lookout.

When Samantha got home, she looked sleepy. She slouched when she set the table for dinner. Her mother told her not to slouch and to stand up straight. Her father said, "You look so tired and we haven't even eaten yet. Are you alright, honey?"

"Sure, I'm fine," she answered. But Samantha was quietly thinking, "Little do they know about sleuthing and how great detectives solve mysteries."

Samantha was tucked into bed quickly after dinner. "It's working," she thought, "I've fooled them. Now, if I can just catch the sock thief."

She got up quietly, switched on her night light, and put her last pair of socks in the center of the room. It was hard to sleep with one eye open, but since Samantha had no sleuth hound, she had to do it. Her open eye scanned the room. Samantha felt like a real sleuth. She was excited to catch the sock burglar.

Suddenly, a big dark shadow appeared on her wall. Scared, Samantha noticed a fuzzy creature entering her room. It looked like a woolly weasel, but it moved like a sloth.

"How strange," she thought, "could this be the sock thief?" Samantha watched the animal creep over to her pair of socks. It smelled them, took one in its mouth, and slinked out of Samantha's room.

Samantha jumped out of bed, threw a small blanket over her sleuth-slouching shoulders, and followed the sock thief. It slowly made its way down the stairs, through the kitchen to the laundry room. The creature revealed unknown powers when it jumped up on the washing machine to leap through a little open window.

Samantha silently slipped out the back door to follow the sock burglar. She was aided by the light of the full moon.

The fuzzy animal stopped by a hole between two bushes near the big cedar tree. Out of the hole popped another woolly creature with three fuzzy babies. They were all glad to see each other.

Then the sock stealer and its mate started tearing Samantha's sock apart and chewing it into tiny bits. They would eat some and feed some to their babies.

Samantha realized that the sock stealer was not a burglar after all. It was just getting food for its family. This fact changed everything. Samantha no longer felt like a sleuth, but like her friendly self.

"Excuse me, I'm Samantha. I live in that house."

The animals were scurrying into their hole.

Samantha said, "Don't go. Please, don't be afraid. I won't hurt you."

The sock stealer turned and stopped.

Samantha went on, "I was so upset about my socks disappearing. Now I see that you use them for food - it's okay! Let's talk and settle this thing as friends. What's your name and what kind of animal are you?"

"My name is Sidney." His family came back out, as he continued, "We're sockeaters."

"Sockeaters? Why, I've never met a sockeater before." Samantha continued, "Why do you only take one sock out of each pair?"

Sidney responded, "Well, it has to do with variety. We all like different flavors. Each color has its own unique taste. Hazel, my wife, loves orange. I like green the best and our kids are fond of brown, pink and blue."

"Gee Sidney, I'm in a lot of trouble because of my missing socks. My mother thinks I lose them and now she won't buy me any more. I'd be willing to help you if you stop taking my socks."

"But, what will we eat?" asked Sidney.

"We're sockatarians," added Hazel.

Samantha asked, "Have you ever tried rags?"

"Yes, but socks smell and taste so delicious!"

"I've got it!" exclaimed Samantha. "I'll put rags in our shoes when we're not wearing them. Each night, I'll set a bowl of smelly rags out by the back door for you."

Sidney, Hazel, and the kids thought this was a grand idea.

Samantha's mother didn't really believe the whole story until the new socks that she bought Samantha remained in pairs and were never lost.

So, if you're forever missing socks, you might try putting some smelly shoe rags in a bowl outside your backdoor at night. Who knows, it might make some sockeaters in your neighborhood very happy.

CASE CLOSED

ZACK'S HARD LESSON

Learning too Early about Discrimination

My name is Zachary Nathan Bromberg, but everyone calls me Zack. It's summertime and I ought to be happy, but I'm not. I'm seven and I feel lousy.

We just moved to Springdale and I don't like it. I miss the big city, its clutter, noises, tall buildings, museums, bustling parks, and the great zoo.

One of the hardest things about moving was leaving behind my friends. Ben, my best pal, lived in our huge apartment building and we attended the same kindergarten and first grade. We played together all the time.

Right after we got here, I had a nightmare. I woke up and it was still dark. My heart was pounding. I was all sweaty and shaking with fright. I dreamt that I'd fallen out of the living room window in our old apartment. It was like I'd been shot out of a canon, dropping 20 floors. Just before I hit the sidewalk, I woke up. At first, I thought I was going to die, but then I realized it was a dream. Yet, I was still scared to death. So I ran into my parents' bedroom and got into their bed. I'm an only child, so they're used to it. They woke up for a short time to comfort me and said, "It's okay; it was just a bad dream." It was like I had gone splat on the concrete, that's how bad it was moving to Springdale.

Over several weeks, the sad and splat feelings went away.

With each passing day, I grew fonder of Springdale. I liked its smallness, friendliness, open spaces, and trees. I could ride my bike nearly anywhere, without my mom fussing at me. I love my new home and my new dog, Lobo. There is a treehouse in my backyard. From the top of it, I can see the whole neighborhood with all its different homes, yards and gardens.

There was only one thing wrong: there were no kids my age to play with. I missed Ben and it hurt deep inside.

My parents said that once I started school I'd make friends with someone else. I had another dream about making friends at my new school. It made me feel better.

As the first day of school approached, I got new clothes and supplies. Even though I was not looking forward to being the new kid at school, I was excited. I liked to learn new things and I knew I'd be with other kids. I even thought maybe my newest dream would come true.

It was the day after Labor Day when I entered Boyd Elementary School. I had butterflies in my stomach, but I held onto my dream and what my parents had told me.

My new school was just the opposite of my old one. It was tiny. The second grade class was very small with only fourteen students. My teacher, Mrs. Henderson, was like a kind grandmother. She said she never had children of her own, so all of us were hers. It felt like I'd found a larger family, one in which I had gobs of brothers and sisters, and all my age!

Mrs. Henderson introduced me first as the only new student. Then she asked each of us to tell about ourselves, our family, things we liked, and what we did during our summer break. I was nervous to go first. "I'm Zack and I moved here this summer from Chicago. My father is a surgeon and my mother helps him in the office. I don't have any brothers or sisters, but I have a big dog named Lobo. It was hard to move and especially to leave my best friend, Ben. It was so sad for a while." I paused and then went on, "I like to ride my bike, play football, basketball, baseball and all kinds of games, but chess and Monopoly are my favorites. I have a neat treehouse in my backyard. I'm happy to be starting school because over the summer I was by myself and bored."

The other kids introduced and talked about themselves. I was most interested by what Chris Johnson had to say. It was weird, his interests and mine were the same. It was like we were identical twins. Chris even liked to play chess and I knew how rare it was for someone to like both football and chess. The tip-off that we might become friends was when Chris said he'd always wanted to play in a treehouse. He was the only one who said that.

During the first recess period, Chris asked me to play football with him and several of his friends. I felt good inside again. Chris and I played together everyday at recess. We asked our parents to take us to school early so we could play before class started. This was all in the first week.

On Sunday, I asked my parents if Chris could come over. They were pleased that I had asked and said, "Any day after school is fine with us."

The next day, I invited Chris to come over after school one day that week.

The following morning before class, Chris didn't seem like himself. He seemed sad. He was strangely quiet and didn't want to play.

I asked, "Are you sick or something?"

Chris answered, "No," but then stumbled over the words, "I can't."

"You can't what?"

Chris replied, "I can't come over to your house to play this week."

I said, "That's okay. You can come over next week."

With watery eyes, Chris sputtered, "I can't ever come over to your house."

I was stunned. "Why not?"

Chris paused and swallowed slowly several times. It was like the words were stuck in his throat and he was having trouble getting them out.

He finally said, "Because you're Jewish."

I questioned him, "Jewish? What are you talking about"

"It's your religion. You're Jewish and I'm Christian. My parents said I can't play with Jews."

I was confused, because I didn't know what he meant.

Chris said he was sorry because he had wanted to come over. He said it was his parents' decision, not his.

I felt funny all day. As if I'd been hit unexpectedly. I felt like I did in the nightmare: like I'd fallen and gone splat. I was mad at Chris's parents because it just wasn't fair.

When I got home, I told my mom what had happened. She gave me a warm hug and soothed my hurt feelings. She seemed upset and it took a lot to get her to be that way. She said something about Chris's parents being prejudiced and that we would talk more about it when my dad came home.

I went outside and Lobo jumped up and gave me a big lick on my cheek. I felt a little better and wished that all people could be as happy and accepting as dogs seemed to be.

When my dad got home, we talked. He said our name was Jewish and that he'd been brought up in the Jewish religion. My father explained that being Jewish went beyond a religion. It was an old culture as well a nation called 'Israel.' He talked about the accomplishments of Jewish people. Dad mentioned only three, but they were people I recognized. George Gershwin, music; Albert Einstein, science; and Sandy Koufax, baseball. My mother said she had always admired Jewish people, but that she had been brought up as a Methodist.

I tried to take it all in, but I still didn't understand.

Then I asked, "You mean Chris couldn't come over to play because I have a Jewish name?"

My parents nodded and explained that some people were prejudiced, in other words, ignorant and hateful without good reason.

I didn't quite get what my parents were talking about, but I knew how I felt. I knew in my heart that it wasn't right and that Chris's parents were wrong. I was so sad that I couldn't hold back my tears. My parents tried to reassure me, "You'll have other friends that can come over to play."

"But Chris is my new best friend and I wanted him to come over."

"We know and we're sorry that this has happened. It's a hard lesson to learn and at such a young age."

As I lay in bed that night, these words kept going through my head, "A hard lesson to learn." I thought that lesson should not have to be learned. I hoped that someday parents would get along as well as children do.

The next two days at school, Chris and I said hello to each other, but we didn't play together. We both needed time to heal. But, the following day, we played at recess. Chris asked me to be on his football team. The day after that, it was rainy so we stayed in at recess time. Chris and I played chess and talked.

I said, "We can still be friends at school."

Chris agreed, and added, "I still feel bad inside about what happened and I'm upset with my parents. I wanted to go over to your house and play and then have you come over to mine."

"I understand and I've been mad at your parents, too. Yesterday, Mrs. Henderson asked me what was going on between us. I shared the whole thing with her. She thought it was great that we were working it out and that I wanted us to remain friends. She said if we could do that, then when we were parents we wouldn't be prejudiced."

I paused and then added, "Mrs. Henderson also saw it as a hard lesson to learn, but said, 'What better place than at school to learn this.'"

It felt good to reconnect with Chris and to maintain our friendship. We both left school that day feeling a whole lot better.

The next morning, I woke up with a big smile on my face. I dreamt that Chris came over after school. We had such a wonderful time chasing Lobo and playing in the treehouse. I thought to myself, "Thank God for dreams."

www.ingramcontent.com/pod-product-compliance
Lightning Source LLC
Chambersburg PA
CBHW070812120626
46557CB00002B/826